George Melville Baker

Past Redemption

A drama in four acts

George Melville Baker

Past Redemption
A drama in four acts

ISBN/EAN: 9783337343835

Printed in Europe, USA, Canada, Australia, Japan

Cover: Foto ©Andreas Hilbeck / pixelio.de

More available books at **www.hansebooks.com**

PAST REDEMPTION.

A DRAMA IN FOUR ACTS.

BY

GEORGE M. BAKER.

BOSTON:

GEORGE M. BAKER AND COMPANY.

1875.

COSTUMES.

John Maynard. Act I. Mixed pants and vest, blue striped shirt, collar rolled over vest, without necktie, straw hat, bald gray wig, heavy gray side-whiskers. Act II. and IV. Add a dark coat.

Harry Maynard. Act I. Neat gray suit, with game-bag, felt hat, leggings, Act III. White shirt without collar, rusty black pants, and coat out at elbows, unshorn face, hollow eyes. Act IV. Light pants, dark vest and coat, with white overcoat, high-colored handkerchief thrown about the neck, felt hat.

Robert Thornton. Act I. Light gray suit, leggings, game-bag, felt hat, heavy watch-chain, and full black beard and moustache. Act II. Handsome black suit, black hat, light overcoat on his arm. Act III. Fashionable suit, with a liberal display of jewelry. Act IV. Dirty black pants, torn at the knee, white shirt, soiled and ragged, showing a red shirt beneath; rough grizzled beard and wig; pale and haggard; dark, ragged coat.

Tom Larcom. Act I. and II. Rough farmer's suit. Act III. Flashy mixed suit, false moustache and chin-whiskers. Act IV. Neat suit with overcoat and felt hat.

Nat Harlow. Neat mixed business suit; a little dandified.

Hanks and Huskers. Farmer's rough suits.

Capt. Bragg. Dark pants, white vest, blue coat with brass buttons, military stock and dickey; tall felt hat; bald gray wig, and military whiskers.

Murdoch. Fashionable dress.

Daley. Dark pants and vest, white apron, sleeves rolled up, no coat.

Stub. Act I. Gray pants, blue striped shirt. Act III. Dark pants, white vest, red necktie, standing collar, black hat, short black coat. Acts II. and IV. Same as first with the addition of a coat.

Mrs. Maynard. Acts I. and II. Cheap calico dress. Act IV. Brown dress. with white apron, collar and cuffs. Gray wig for all.

Charity, age about thirty-five. Act II. Pretty muslin dress, with a white apron, tastefully trimmed, lace cap, light wig. Act III..Gray dress handsomely trimmed, gray waterproof cloak. Act III. Dark travelling dress, handsome cloak and hat.

Jessie. Act I. Muslin dress, with collar and cuffs. Act II. Something of the same kind. Act III. Handsome dress of light color. Act IV. Gray travelling dress, with cloak and hat.

Kitty. Act I. Light muslin dress. Act II. Something of the same kind. Act IV. Red dress, white collar and cuffs, shawl and hat.

Chorus of Ladies for Act III. Dark and light dresses, with "clouds" of different colors about their heads.

PAST REDEMPTION.

A DRAMA IN FOUR ACTS.

———◆———

ACT I.—A HUSKING AT THE OLD HOME.

SCENE.—*A barn. In flat, large door to roll back* L., *closed; above door, hay-mow, practicable staging, loose hay piled upon it; over that, window, through which moonbeams stream.* L., *stalls with harness suspended from pegs, bench on which are two basins and towels.* R., *bins, above stalls and bins,* R. *and* L., *hay-mow with hay (painted).* R. C.,

two benches thus : B D C A *, on which are seated* A.

TOM LARCOM, B. NAT HARLOW, *and between them four farmers, three girls; another girl standing* C.; *beside her on floor, kneeling, a farmer picks up the husks thrown by the huskers, and puts them in a basket. A small pile of corn,* D., *which the occupants of the benches are at work on, throwing the corn into bins,* R.; *the husks behind. Just back of* B, HANKS *seated on a barrel with violin playing,* "*In the sweet by and by.*" STUB *leaning against wing,* L., I E. *listening; stool* R., I E.; *red lanterns hung* R. *and* L., *red light from footlights.* HANKS *plays the air through during the rising of curtain.*

STUB. Golly! hear dat now, will you? D-d-dat what I call music in de har, fur it jes make my har stan' on end, yes, it does. And I feel—I feel jes as dough I was skewered onto dat ar fiddle-bow, an' bein' drawed frou a sea ob bilin' merlasses. Golly, so sweet!

NAT. There's a first-class puff for you, Hanks, from the mouth of a critic—with a black border.

TOM. You do beat all nater, Hanks, with the fiddle; your hand is as cute, and your ear as fine, as though the one had never held a plough, or the other listened to the jingling of a cowbell. Talk of your genuses. Give me the chap that's a Jack at any thing, from digging ninety tater-hills afore breakfast, to sparking a pretty girl at 'leven o'clock on a starlight night. .

STUB. Wid de ole man comin' roun' de corner ob de house wid a double-barrel rebolver, "You scoot or I shoot." Don't ͵forget de embellishments, Tom Larcom. (*All laugh.*)

NAT. Ha, ha! had you there, Tom. .

TOM. What are you laughing at? If old Corum mistook me for a prowler one night, am I to blame?

STUB. Coorse not, coörse not, when you didn't stop to 'lucidate, but jumped de fence and scooted down d'e road hollering "Murder!" (*Laugh.*)

TOM (*flinging an ear of corn at* STUB). A little more ear and less tongue, Stub.

STUB (*ducking his head*). Don't waste de fodder. Had ear enough dat night. Golly! jes woke de whole neighborhood.

TOM. Ah! the course of true love never did run smooth.

STUB. By golly! you — you found it pretty smoove runnin' dat night. .

TOM (*threatening* STUB). Will you be quiet?

· STUB. Ob coorse. Don't waste de fodder.

NAT. Ah, Tom, Nature never cut you out for a lover.

TOM. P'r'aps not; but I've got *art* enough to cut you out, Nat, if you do make up to my property, Kitty Corum. (*Enter* KITTY, R., *overhearing last words.*)

KITTY. Indeed! Your property! I like that. And when, pray, did you come into possession?

TOM. That's for you to say, Kitty. I'm an expectant heir as yet. Don't forget me in your will, Kitty.

NAT. Don't write your will in his favor.

KITTY.   "When a woman wills she wills: depend on't;
             And when she won't she won't, and there's the end on't."

TOM (*sings*). "If I could write my title clear."

NAT. Give me the title, Kitty.

TOM. I'd give you a title — Counter-jumper, Yardstick; that's about your measure. You talk about titles: why, all you are good for is to measure tape and ribbons, cut "nigger-head," shovel sugar, and peddle herrings for old Gleason. Bah! I smell soap now.

NAT (*jumping up*). You just step outside, and you shall smell brimstone, and find your measure on the turf, Tom Larcom.

KITTY. There, there, stop that! I'll have no quarrelling. Supper's nearly ready, and the corn not finished.

TOM. We'll be ready for the supper, Kitty. If I could only find a red ear.

KITTY. And if you could?

TOM. I should make an impression on those red lips of yours that would astonish you.

KITTY. Indeed! It would astonish me more if you had the chance. (*Laugh.*) But where's Harry Maynard?

TOM. Off gunning with Mr. Thornton. He said he'd be back in time for the husking: they must have lost their way.

KITTY. His last night at home, too.

STUB. Yas, indeed. Off in de mornin', afore de broke ob day. I's gwine to drive dem ober to de steam-jine station. Miss Jennie gwine to see him off; 'spect she'll jes cry her eyes out comin' home.

TOM. Well, I can't see the use of Harry Maynard's trottin' off to the city with this Mr. Thornton. Let well enough alone, say I. Here's a good farm, and a smart, pretty girl ready to share life with him; and yet off he goes to take risks in something he knows nothing about.

KITTY. Don't say a word against Mr. Thornton; he's just splendid.

CHORUS OF GIRLS. Oh, elegant!

TOM. There it is! Vanity and vexation! here's a man old enough to be your father. Comes up here in his fine clothes, with a big watch-chain across his chest, and a seal ring on his finger, and you girls are dead in love with him at first sight.

KITTY. Tom, you're jealous. Harry Maynard is not content to settle down here; he wants to see the world, and I like his spunk. If I was a man *I* would get the polish of city life.

STUB. So would I, so would I. Yas, indeed; get de polish down dar. Look at Joe Trash; he went down dar, he did. New suit ob store clo's onto him, and forty dollars in his calf-skin. He come back in free days polished right out ob his boots.

TOM. Well, I s'pose it's out of fashion not to like this Thornton, but there's something in the twist of his waxed-end mustache, and the roll of his eye, that makes me feel bad for Harry.

KITTY. You needn't fear for Harry. He won't eat him.

STUB. No, sir, he's not a connubial : he's a gemblum.

TOM. Ah! here's the last ear, and, by jingo! it's a red one.

CHORUS. Good for you, Tom! good for you!

NAT. I'll give you a dollar for your chance.

TOM. No, you don't, Nat; I'm in luck. — Now, Kitty, I claim the privilege. A kiss for the finder of the red ear. (*All rise.*)

KITTY. Not from me, saucebox.

NAT. Run, Kitty, run! (KITTY *runs in and out among the huskers,* TOM *in pursuit.*)

TOM. It's no use, Kitty; you can't escape me. (*She runs down* R. *corner; as* TOM *is about to seize her, she stoops, and runs across stage, catches* STUB *by the arms, and whirls him round.* TOM, *in pursuit, clasps* STUB *in his arms.*)

STUB. "I'd offer thee dis cheek ob mine." If you want a smack take it. I won't struggle.

TOM (*strikes his face with hand*). How's that for a smack?

STUB. Dat's de hand widout de heart: takes all de bloom out ob my complexion. (*Goes across stage holding on to his face, and exits* R. KITTY *runs through crowd again, comes* R., TOM *in pursuit.*)

TOM. It's no use, Kitty: you must pay tribute.

KITTY. Never, never! (*Runs across to* L., *and then up stage to back. Door opens, and enter* HARRY MAYNARD *and* THORNTON, *equipped with guns and game-bags;* KITTY *runs into* HARRY'S *arms.*)

HARRY. Hallo! just in time. You've the red ear, Tom, so, as your friend, I'll collect the tribute. (*Kisses* KITTY.)

KITTY (*screams*). How dare you, Harry Maynard!

TOM. Yes, Harry Maynard, how dare you?

(THORNTON, HARRY, KITTY, TOM, *and* NAT *come down; others carry back the benches, and clear the stage; then converse in groups at back.*)

HARRY. Don't scold, Tom. It's the first game that has crossed my path to-day: the first shot I've made. So the corn is husked, and I not here to share your work. We've had a long tramp, and lost our way (*goes to* R. *with* THORN-TON; *they divest themselves of their bags, and lean their guns against bin.* 2d *entrance.*)

TOM (L. C.). Empty bags! Well, you are smart gunners: not even a rabbit.

HARRY (R. C. THORNTON *sits on stool*, R.). No, Tom; they were particularly shy to-day, so I had to content myself with a deer, your dear, Tom. (*All laugh;* NAT, L., *very loud,* TOM *threatening him.*)

KITTY (C.). His dear, indeed! I'll have you to under-stand I'm not to be made game of.

HARRY. No, dear, no one shall make game of you; but keep a sharp lookout, for there's a keen hunter on the track, and when Tom Larcom flings the matrimonial noose —

KITTY. He may be as lucky as you have been to-day, and return empty-handed.

TOM. Don't say that, Kitty; haven't I been your de-voted —

KITTY. Fiddlesticks! (*pushes him back, and comes to* L. C.) If there is any thing I hate, it's sparking before com-pany.

NAT (L.). And there's where you're right, Kitty. As much as I love you, I would never dare to be so outspoken before company.

TOM. Oh, you're a smart one, you are! (*Enter* STUB, R.)

STUB. Supper's onto de table, and Miss Maynard, she says, says she, you're to come right into de kitchen, eat all you like, drink all you like, an' smash all de dishes if you like; an' dere's fourteen kinds ob pies, an' turnobers, an' turn-unders, an' cold chicken, an' — an' — cheese —

HARRY. That will do, Stub. My good mother is a boun-tiful provider, and needs no herald. So, neighbors, take your partners; Hanks will give you a march, and Mr. Thornton and I will join you as soon as we have removed the marks of the forlorn chase.

STUB. Yas, Massa Hanks, strike up a march: some-thing lively. Dead march in Saul; dat's fus rate.

TOM (C.). Kitty, shall I have the pleasure? (*Offers his left arm to* KITTY.)

NAT (L.). Miss Corum, shall I have the honor? (*Offers his right arm to* KITTY.)

KITTY (*between them, looks at each one, turns up her*

nose at TOM, *and takes* NAT'S *arm*).   Thank you, Mr.
Harlow.   I'll intrust this *property* to you.

NAT.   For life, Kitty?

KITTY.   On a short lease.   (*They go up* C., *face audience;
others pair, and fall in behind them.*)

TOM (C.).   Cut,—a decided cut.   I must lay in wait for
Yardstick when this breaks up, and I think he will need
about a pound of beefsteak for his eyes in the morning.
(*Goes* L. *and leans dejectedly against wing.   Music strikes
up, the march is made across stage once, and off* R., STUB
strutting behind.)

HARRY (*crosses* L.).   Why, Tom, don't you go in?

TOM.   Certainly.   Come, Hanks.   (*Goes over to* HANKS.)
They'll want your music in there, and I'm just in tune to
play second fiddle.   (*They exeunt* R., *arm in arm.*)

HARRY (*goes to bench* L., *and washes hands*).   Now, Mr.
Thornton, for a wash, and then we'll join them.   (THORNTON
keeps his seat in a thoughtful attitude. HARRY *comes
down.*)   Hallo! what's the matter?   Homesick?

THORNTON (*laughs*).   Not exactly; but there's something in this old barn, these merry huskers, this careless
happy life you farmers lead, has stirred up old memories,
until I was on the point of breaking out with that melancholy
song, "Oh, would I were a boy again!"

HARRY.   Now, don't be melancholy.   That won't chime
with the dear old place; for, though it has not been free
from trouble, we drive all care away with willing hands and
cheerful hearts.

THORNTON.   It is a cheery old place, and so reminds
me of one I knew when I was young; for, like you, I was a
farmer's boy.

HARRY.   Indeed! you never told me that.

THORNTON.   No: for 'tis no fond recollection to me, and
I seldom refer to it.   I did not take kindly to it, so early
forsook a country life for the stir and bustle of crowded
cities.   But, when one has reached the age of forty, 'tis
time to look back.

HARRY.   Not with regret, I trust: for you tell me you
have acquired wealth in mercantile pursuits, and so pictured
the busy life of the city, that I am impatient to carve my
fortune there.

THORNTON.   And you are right.   The strong-armed,
clear-brained wanderers from the country carry off the grand

prizes there. You are ambitious: you shall rise; and, when you are forty, revisit these scenes, a man of wealth and influence.

HARRY. Ah, Mr. Thornton, when one has a friend like you to lead the way, success is certain. I am proud of your friendship, and thankfully place my future in your keeping.

THORNTON. That shows keen wit at the outset. Trust me, and you shall win. (*Rises.*) But I am keeping you from your friends, and I know a pair of bright eyes are anxiously looking for you. (*Goes to bench, and washes hands.*)

JESSIE (*outside* L., *sings*),—

> " In the sweet by and by,
> We shall meet on that beautiful shore," &c.

HARRY. Ah! my "sweet by and by" is close at hand. (*Enter* JESSIE, R., *with pail.*)

JESSIE. O you truant! (*Runs to him.*) Now, don't flatter yourself that I came in search of you. Do you see this pail? this is my excuse.

HARRY. 'Tis an empty one, Jessie. I am very sorry you have been anxious on my account; but I'm all ready, so let's in to supper.

JESSIE. Not so fast, sir: the pail must be filled. I'm going for milk.

HARRY. Then "I'll go with you, 'my pretty maid."—You'll excuse me a moment, Mr. Thornton.

JESSIE. Mr. Thornton!—Dear me, I didn't see you! Good evening.

THORNTON. Good evening, Miss Jessie.

JESSIE. Are you very, very hungry?

THORNTON. Oh, ravenous! ·

JESSIE. Then don't wait, but hurry in, or I won't be responsible for your supper: huskers are such a hungry set.—Come, Harry.

HARRY. Don't wait, Mr. Thornton: it takes a long time to get the milk; don't it, Jessie?

JESSIE. Not unless you tease me—but you always do.

HARRY. Of course, I couldn't help it; and tease and milk go well together. (*Exeunt* JESSIE *and* HARRY, L. THORNTON *stands* C. *looking after them.*)

THORNTON. Yes, yes, 'tis a cheery old place. Pity the storm should ever beat upon it; pity that dark clouds should ever obscure its brightness; yet they will come. For the first time in a life of passion and change, this rural beauty has stirred my heart with a longing it never felt before. I cannot analyze it. The sound of her voice thrills me; the sight of her face fascinates me; the touch of her hand maddens me; and, with it all, the shadow of some long-forgotten presence mystifies me. This must be love. For I would dare all, sacrifice all, to make her mine. She is betrothed to him. He must be taken from her side, made unworthy of her, made to forget her. The task is easy to one skilled in the arts of temptation. Once free, her heart may be turned towards me. 'Tis a long chase: no wonder I am melancholy, Harry Maynard; but there's a keen, patient hunter on the track, who never fails, never. (*Enter* JOHN MAYNARD, R.)

JOHN MAYNARD. Well, well, here's hospitality: here's hospitality with a vengeance. That rascal Harry has deserted you, has he? — you, our honored guest. It's too bad, too bad.

THORNTON. Don't give yourself any uneasiness about me, old friend. Harry has left me a moment to escort a young lady.

MAYNARD. Ah, yes, I understand: Jessie, our Jessie, the witch that brings us all under her spells. No wonder the boy forgot his manners; but to desert you —

THORNTON. Don't speak of desertion; you forget I am one of the family.

MAYNARD. I wish you were with all my heart. I like you, Mr. Thornton. I flatter myself I know a gentleman, when I meet him. You came up here, looked over my stock, and bought my horses at my own price, no beating down, no haggling; and I said to myself, He's a gentleman, for gentlemen never haggle. So I say I like you (*gives his hand*), and that's something to remember, for John Maynard don't take kindly to strangers.

THORNTON. I trust I shall always merit your good opinion.

MAYNARD. Of course you will; you can't help it. There's our Harry just raves about you, and you've taken a fancy to him. I like you for that too. Then you are going to take him away, and show him the way to fortune by your high pressure, bustle and rush, city ways. Not just the notion I wanted to get into his head; but he's ambitious, and I'll not stand in his way. He's our only boy now. There was

another; he went down at the call of his country, a brave,
noble fellow, and fell among the first; and he died bravely:
he couldn't help it, for he was a Maynard. But 'twas a hard
blow to us. It made us lonely here; and even now, when
the wind howls round the old house in the cold winter
nights, mother and I sit silent in the corner, seeing our boy's
bright face in the fire, till the tears roll down her cheeks,
and I — I set my teeth together, and clasp her hands, and
whisper, He died bravely, mother, — died for his country like
a hero, — like a hero.

THORNTON. Ah! 'tis consoling to remember that.

MAYNARD. Yes, yes. And now the other, our only boy,
goes forth to fight another battle, full of temptation and
danger. Heaven grant him a safe return!

THORNTON. Amen to that! But fear not for him. I
have a regard, yes, call it a fatherly regard; and it shall be
my duty to guard him among the temptations of the city.

MAYNARD. That's kind; that's honest. I knew you
were a gentleman, and I trust you freely.

THORNTON. You shall have a good account of him; and
'twill not be lonely here, for you have a daughter left to
comfort you.

MAYNARD. Our Jessie, bless her! she's a treasure.
Sixteen years ago, on one of the roughest nights, our
Harry, then a mere boy, coming up from the village, found
a poor woman and her babe on the road lying helpless in the
snow. He brought her here: we recognized her, as the
daughter of one of our neighbors, a girl who had left home,
and found work in the city. This was her return. Her
unnatural father shut the door in her face, and she wandered
about until found by Harry. She lingered through the
night, speechless, and died at sunrise. I sought the father,
but he had cast her out of his heart and home; for he believed her to be a wanton. Indignant at his cruelty, I struck
him down; for I'm mighty quick-tempered, and can't stand a
mean argument. I gave the mother Christian burial, took
the child to my heart, and love her as if she was my own.
As for him, public opinion drove him from our village; and
her child is loved and honored as he could never hope to be.

THORNTON. And your son will marry her with this
stain upon her?

MAYNARD. Stain? what stain? Upon her mother's
finger was a plain gold ring; and, though the poor thing's

lips were silent, her eyes wandered to that ring with a mean-
ing none could fail to guess. She was a deserted wife; and;
even had she been all her father thought her, what human
being has a right to be relentless, when we should forgive
as we all hope to be forgiven? But come, here I am chatting
away like an old maid at a quilting. Come in, and get your
supper, for you must be hungry: come in. (*Exeunt* R.
Enter L., HARRY, *with his arm round* JESSIE, *the pail in
his hand.*)

HARRY.   Yes, Jessie, 'tis hard to leave you behind; but
our parting will not be for long.   Once fairly embarked in
my new life, with a fair chance of success before me, I shall
return to seek my ready helper.

JESSIE.   Harry, perhaps you will think me foolish, but I
tremble at your venture.   Why seek new paths to fortune
when here is all that could make our lives happy and con-
tented?

HARRY.   But it's so slow, Jessie; and, with the best of
luck, I should be but a plodding farmer.   To plough and dig,
sow and reap, year in and year out, — 'tis a hard life, all
bone and muscle : to be sure, rugged health and deep sleep;
but *there* is excitement and bustle, quick success and rousing
fortunes.   Ah, Jessie, if one half my schemes work well,
you shall be a lady.

JESSIE.   To be your own true, loving wife, your ever
ready helper, is all I ask.   O Harry, if you should forget
me in all this bustle !

HARRY.   Forget you? Never: in all my hopes you are
the shining light; in all my air-built castles, which energy
should make real and substantial ones, you are enthroned
my queen.

JESSIE.   Enthrone me in your heart: let me be an influence there, to shield you from temptation, and, come fortune
or failure, I shall be content.

HARRY.   An influence, Jessie : hear my confession.   Un-
known to you, I stood beneath your window last night, as
you sat looking up at the moon, singing the song I love, " In
the sweet by and by."   I thought how soon we must part,
and your sweet voice brought tears to my eyes.   Jessie, I
believe, that, were I so weak as to fall beneath temptation,
in the darkest hour of misery, the remembrance of that
voice would call me back to you and a better life.

JESSIE.   You will not forget me?

HARRY. Oh, we are getting melancholy. (*Smiles.*) Why should *I* not fear a rival?

JESSIE. Now you are jesting, Harry. Do I not owe my life to you?

HARRY. Hush, hush! that is a forbidden subject, and all you owe to me has been paid with interest in the gift of your true, loving heart. (*They pass off,* R. *Enter* CAPT. BRAGG, C.)

CAPT. BRAGG. Well, I never — no, never. If Parson Broadnose himself, in full black, with all his theological prognostications to back him, had said to me, Capt. Bragg, did you ever? I should have fixed my penetrating eyes upon him, and answered boldly, No, never. Slighted, absolutely, undeniably, unquestionably slighted! I, Capt. Nathan Bragg, distinguished for my martial deportment, my profound knowledge, my ready wit, yes, every thing that adds a charm to merrymaking; I, ex-commander of that illustrious corps, the Lawless Rangers, that rivals the grandest European regiments in drill and parade, — slighted at a mean, contemptible little husking. Fact, by jingo! But I'm not to be slighted: I won't be slighted. I am here to testify my profound contempt for a slight. If John Maynard has a husking, and forgets to invite the grand central figure on such occasions, it is the duty of the grand central figure to overlook the little breach of etiquette, and appear to contribute to the happiness of its fellow townsmen. There is an air of gloom about this place, all owing to my absence. They're in to supper: I'll join them, to cheer the dull hearts and (*going* R.)— Hallo! guns, guns. (*Takes up one.*) There's a beauty. This reminds me of my warlike days at country muster, and the Lawless Rangers. Ah, those rangers! every man with a Roman nose, six feet high, and a dead shot: not a man would miss the dead eye at one hundred paces, — if he could help it. Ah! I can see 'em now as I gave the order: ready — aim — fire (*raising gun and firing as he speaks.*) Murder! the blasted thing was loaded. (*Drops it, and staggers across stage to* L., *trembling. A fowl drops from* R., *at the shot. Enter* R., MR. MAYNARD, STUB, HARRY, JESSIE, TOM, *and* MRS. MAYNARD.)

MAYNARD. Who fired that gun? Ah, Capt. Bragg, what's the matter?

STUB (*taking up fowl*). Dat ar poor ole rooster am a gone goose. Dat's what's de matter.

HARRY (*taking up gun*). Captain, have you been meddling with my gun?

MRS. MAYNARD. Of course he has: he's always meddling.

CAPT. Mrs. Maynard, that's an absurd remark. It's all right: one of my surprises. You must know I wanted a rooster for to-morrow's dinner. I'm very fond of them: there's such a warlike taste about them. And we are a little short of roosters; my last one, being a little belligerent this morning, walked into Higgins's yard, and engaged in deadly combat: so deadly that Higgins's fowl was stretched a lifeless corse upon the ground: for Bragg's roosters always lick, always. But in spite of my earnest protest, despite the warlike maxim, Spoils to the victor belong, Higgins shot my rooster and nailed him to his barn door like a crow, and *his* crow was gone. Fact, by jingo.

MAYNARD. Yes: but what's that got to do with my rooster?

CAPT. Well, I wanted a rooster: so says I to myself, Maynard's got plenty, he can spare one just as well as not; so I'm come to borrow one. Well, I found you had company, and not wishing to disturb you, and seeing a gun handy, I singled out my dinner roosting aloft there, raised the gun, — you know I'm a dead shot, — shut my eyes —

TOM. Shut your eyes! Is that one of your dead shot tactics?

CAPT. Shut one eye, squinted, of course, that's what I said, and fired. The result of that shot is before you. If you will-examine that fowl, you will find that he is shot clean through the neck.

STUB. He's shot all ober; looks jes for all de world like a huckleberry puddin'.

MAYNARD. Well, captain, I call this rather a cool proceeding.

CAPT. Ah, you flatter me: but coolness is a characteristic of the Braggs. When I raised that company for the war, the Lawless Rangers, I said to those men, Be cool: don't let your ardor carry you too far.

TOM. Yours didn't run you into battle, did it, captain?

CAPT. I couldn't run anywhere. Just when the call came for those men, after I had prepared them for battle, and longed to lead them to the field, rheumatism — in the legs too — blasted all my hopes, and left me behind. But my soul was with them, and, if they achieved distinction, they owed it all to my early teaching — to the Bragg they left behind. (*Struts up stage.*)

JOHN MAYNARD (*to* THORNTON). Ah! he's a sly old fox.

THORNTON (*tapping his head*). A little wrong here.

MAYNARD. No, he's a cool, calculating man, but as vain as a peacock.

CAPT. (*coming down*). Sorry I didn't know you had company. Wouldn't have intruded for the world.

MAYNARD. It's all right, captain. Join us: we were expecting you. (*To* THORNTON.) I can say that truly, for he's always popping in where he's not wanted.

CAPT. Ah! thank you. A-husking, I see. What's the yield?

MAYNARD. Excellent. My five-acre lot has given me two hundred bushels. That's what I call handsome.

CAPT. Pooh! you should see my corn. There's nothing like Bragg's corn. My three-acre lot gave me three hundred bushels, and every other ear was a red one.

CHORUS. Oh!

CAPT. Fact, by jingo! (NAT *and* KITTY *enter* R., *followed by huskers.*)

MAYNARD. Come, boys, get ready for the dance. — Mother, you take the captain in to supper.

MRS. MAYNARD. Come, captain, you must be hungry.

CAPT. (*coming to* R.). Thank you, I could feed a bit. But don't stir: I can find the table; and, when I do find it, I shall do full justice to your fare, or I am no Bragg. (*Exit* R. HARRY *rolls back the big door, others put out lanterns. Moonlight streams upon the floor. Change footlights.*)

THORNTON (*to* JESSIE). Miss Jessie, shall I have the honor of dancing with you?

JESSIE. Thank you, Mr. Thornton. (*Takes his arm, and they go up.* NAT *and* KITTY *come down* C.)

NAT. Ah, Kitty, now for the dance. Of course you will open the ball with me.

KITTY (*hanging on his arm, looks around, and nods to* TOM; *he comes down on the other side*). Did I promise you a dance to-night, Mr. Larcom?

TOM (*sulkily*). I believe you did: but I ain't particular.

KITTY. But I am.

NAT. Kitty, dance with me.

KITTY. I shall do just as Mr. Larcom says; if he does not wish me, why —

Tom. Oh, Kitty, you know I do, you know I do! (*Takes her arm, and whirls her up stage. NAT goes over to L., and leans against wing watching them.*)   .

Harry. Now, boys, take your partners for Hull's Victory. — Come, mother. (*Gives* Mrs. Maynard *his arm, and goes to door, taking the lead.* Tom *and* Kitty, Thornton *and* Jessie *next, others form in front of them.* Stub *goes to* L. *Dance, Hull's Victory. When* Tom *and* Kitty *come in front,* Tom *talks with* Mr. Maynard, *who stands* R., *and* Kitty *makes signs to* Nat: *he comes over, takes her arm, and they go up and off,* L. U. E., *appearing soon after in the loft at back; they sit on the hay, and watch the dancing. The dance is continued some time,* Stub *dancing by himself,* L. *When it is* Tom's *turn to dance,* Stub *slips into set, and gives his hand.* Tom *dances a little while before finding his mistake; then pushes* Stub *back, looks round and up, descries* Kitty *and* Nat. *Goes off* L. U. E. *Dance goes on. Enter* Capt. Bragg, R., *with a chicken-bone in one hand, and a piece of pie in the other; stands watching the dancers.* Tom *appears in loft, behind* Nat. Nat *puts his arm round* Kitty, *and is about to kiss her;* Tom *pulls him back upon the hay, and pummels him.*)

Nat. Help! Murder! Murder! (*Dance stops.*)

Capt. Hallo! Thieves! Burglars! (*Seizes the other gun, raises it, and fires. Fowl drops from* L. Stub *picks it up;* Mr. Maynard *seizes* Captain's *arm.*)

Stub. Dere's anoder rooster dead shot.

Capt. Fact, by jingo!

Tableau.

Capt. R. C., *with gun raised;* Maynard C., *with hand on gun;* Stub L., *holding up fowl; others starting forward watching group.* Tom *has* Nat *down in the loft with fist raised above him.* Kitty *kneels* R. *of them, with her apron to her face.*

Curtain.

ACT II. — PAST REDEMPTION.

Exterior of MAYNARD'S *farm-house. House on* R. *with porch covered with vines; fence running across stage at back, with gateway* C., *backed by road and landscape.* L.C., *large tree, with bench running round its trunk; trees* L. *Time, sunset. Enter* TOM *from* L., *through gate, a bunch of flowers in his hand.*

TOM. The same old errand: chasing that will-o'-wisp, Kitty Corum, — she who is known as the girl with two strings to her bow; who has one hand for Tom Larcom and another for Nat Harlow, and no heart for either. I'm the laughing-stock of the whole neighborhood; but misery loves company, and Nat is in the same box. If she would only say No, and have done with it, I believe I should be happy, especially if Nat received the "No." She won't let either of us go. But she must. To-night I'll speak for the last time; I'll pop. If she takes me, well: if not, I'll pop off and leave the field to Nat. Luckily I found out she was to help Mrs. Maynard to-day. Nat hasn't heard of it, and no doubt he's trudging off to old Corum's. Here she comes. Lay there, you beauties! (*Puts flowers on bench.*) Kitty will know what that means. (*Exit* L. *Enter* KITTY *from house.*)

KITTY. What a nice woman Mrs. Charity Goodall is, to be sure! so graceful and sweet, not a bit like her big rough brother, John Maynard. But then, she's learned the city ways. A widow, poor thing — and not so poor, either; for her husband, when he died, left her a consolation in the shape of a very handsome fortune. (*Sees flowers.*) I declare, somebody's attentions are really overpowering. No matter where I am, either at home or abroad, when night comes I always find a bunch of flowers placed in my way. Of

19

course these are for me: no one would think of offering
flowers to Jessie.   Poor Jessie! 'tis eighteen months since
Harry Maynard left home, and six months since a line has
been received from him.   Ah, well! this comes of having
but one string to your bow.   I manage matters differently.
(*Sits on bench. Enter* NAT *from* L., *through gate; steps
behind tree.*)   Now, I really would like to know who is so
attentive, so loving, as to send me these pretty flowers.
  NAT (*sticks his head round tree,* R.).   And can't you
guess, Kitty?
  KITTY (*starting*).   O Nat!
  TOM (*sticks his head out from* L. *Aside.*)   O Nat! indeed, you owe Nat nothing for flowers.   The mean sneak!
(*Retires.*)
  NAT (*coming forward*).   Now, this is what I call luck,
Kitty.   I heard you were here, and I think I've taken the
wind out of Tom Larcom's sails to-night.   No doubt he's
tramping off to your house to find nobody at home.   Ha,
ha! had him there.   (TOM *creeps out, and gets behind tree.*)
  KITTY.   And so I am indebted to you for all these pretty
flowers.
  NAT.   Oh! never mind the posies, Kitty.   I have some-
thing very serious to say to you to-night.   (*Sits beside her* R.)
  KITTY.   Very, very serious, Nat?
  NAT.   As serious, Kitty, as though I were a prisoner at
the bar waiting my sentence.
  TOM.   Ah! in that case, there should be a full bench,
Kitty.   (*Comes round and sits on bench,* L.)
  NAT.   The deuce!   Tom Larcom, what brought you
here?
  TOM.   I came to court; that is, to see justice done you.
  NAT.   You be hanged!
  TOM.   Thank you: let that be your fate; and I'll be
transported.   (*Puts his arm round* KITTY'S *neck.*)
  KITTY.   How dare you, Tom Larcom?   (*Pushes off his
arm.*)
  TOM.   It's "neck or nothing" with me to-night, Kitty.
  NAT.   Tom, you are taking unfair advantage of me.
  TOM.   Am I?   How about Kitty's posies, Nat, that I
laid upon the bench?
  KITTY.   It's you, then, Tom.— O Nat! how could you?
  NAT.   I didn't: I only asked you a conundrum.   All's
fair in love.   What's a few flowers, any way?   Why, Kitty,
smile upon me, and you shall have a garden.

Tom. Yes, a kitchen garden, with you as the central figure, — a cabbage-head.

Nat. Kitty, you must listen to me. I have a serious question to ask you.

Tom. So have I, Kitty.

Kitty. You too, Tom? A pair of serious questions! Shall I get out my handkerchief?

Nat. Kitty, I have sought you for the last time.

Tom. Thank Heaven!

Nat. Perhaps —

Tom. O, Kitty, give him your blessing, and let him depart!

Nat. I am on the point of leaving —

Tom. Good-by, old fellow. You have our fondest wishes where'er you go. "'Tis absence makes the heart grow fonder" —

Nat. — Of leaving my fate in your hands.

Tom. Oh, this is touching!

Nat. 'Tis now two years since I commenced paying attention to you.

Kitty. Stop, Nat. This is a serious business: let us be exact, — one year and ten months.

Tom. Correct. I remember it from the circumstance that I had, about a month before, singled you out as the object of my adoration.

Nat. "We met by chance."

Tom. "The usual way." Oh come, Nat, do be original!

Nat. I worshipped the very ground you trod on —

Tom. And I the shoes you trod in: that's one step higher.

Nat. From that time —

Kitty. One year and ten months.

Nat. From that time I have loved you sincerely, devotedly, and —

Tom. *Etcettery.* Same here, Kitty, with a dictionary thrown in.

Nat. You have become very, very dear to me, Kitty.

Tom. You are enshrined in this bosom, Kitty.

Nat. Without you, my life would be miserable — a desert.

Tom. And mine without you, Kitty, a Saharah.

Nat. I have waited long to gain your serious attention, to ask you to be my wife. Now is the appointed time.

TOM (*takes out watch*).   Fifteen minutes after seven : the very time I appointed.

NAT.   Let me hear my sentence.

TOM.   Put me out of misery.

KITTY.   This is indeed serious.   Am I to understand that you have both reached that point in courtship when a final answer is required?

NAT.   That's exactly the point I have reached.

TOM.   It's "going, going, gone " with me.

KITTY.   You will both consider my answer final?

BOTH.   We will.

KITTY.   No quarrelling, no teasing, no appeal?

NAT.   None. (*Aside.*) I'm sure of her.

TOM.   Never. (*Aside.*) Nat's sacked, certain.

KITTY.   Very well.   Your attentions, Mr. Harlow, have been very flattering, — your presents handsome.

NAT.   Well, I'm not a bad-looking —

KITTY.   I mean the presents you have bestowed upon me, — calicoes of the latest patterns, sweetmeats in great varieties, which you, as a shopkeeper, have presented me with.

TOM (*aside*).   At old Gleason's expense.

KITTY.   Of course I value them.   But a girl wants the man she loves to be a hero : to plunge into rivers to rescue drowning men, and all that sort of thing.

TOM (*aside*).   And Nat can't swim.   That's hard on him.

KITTY.   And you, Mr. Larcom, have been equally attentive.   Your gifts — the choicest fruits of your orchard, the beautiful flowers nightly laid within my reach — all have a touching significance.   Still, as I said, a girl looks for something higher in the man she loves.·   He must be bold —

NAT (*aside*).   Tom's afraid of his own shadow.   He's mittened.

KITTY.   Rush into burning houses, stop runaway horses, rescue distressed females ; and I am very much afraid neither of my devoted admirers can claim the title of hero.   So, gentlemen, with many thanks for your attentions, I say No.

NAT.   No!   That is for Tom.

TOM.   No!   You mean Nat.

KITTY.   I mean both. (NAT *and* TOM *look at her, then at each other, then both rise and come front.*)

NAT.   Tom.

TOM. Nat.

NAT. You've got the sack.

TOM. You've got the mitten.

NAT. She's a flirt.

TOM. A coquette.

NAT. I shall never speak to her again.

TOM. Henceforth she and I are strangers. (*They shake hands, then turn and go up to her.*)

BOTH. Kitty!

KITTY. Remember, no appeal. (*They look at her ruefully, then come down.*)

NAT. Tom, I bear you no ill-will. Are you going my way?

TOM. Nat, you are the best fellow in the world. I'm going in to see John Maynard.

NAT. We shall be friends.

TOM. In despair, yes. (*They shake hands.* NAT *goes up to gate,* TOM *goes to door* R.)

NAT. Good-by, Kitty. I shall never see you again. I'm going across the river. Should any accident happen, look kindly upon my remains. (*Goes off* L.)

TOM. Good-by, Kitty. I'm going in to borrow one of John Maynard's razors; they are very sharp. Should I happen to cut any thing, don't trouble yourself to call the doctor. (*Exit into house.*)

KITTY. Ha, ha, ha! They'll never trouble me, never. They'll be back before I can count ten. One, two, three, four, five — (NAT *appears* L., *comes to gate.* TOM *comes from house: they see each other, turn and run back.*) I knew it. The silly noodles! here they are again. (*Enter* JESSIE, *from house.*) Didn't I tell you my answer was final? and here you are again.

JESSIE. Why, Kitty, are you dreaming?

KITTY (*jumping up*). Bless me, Jessie, is that you?

JESSIE. Have you seen Stub? has he returned from the office? Ah! here he is. (*Enter* STUB, L., *through gate, dejectedly.* JESSIE *runs up to him.*) O Stub, have you brought no letter?

STUB. Jes none at all, Miss Jessie; dat ar' post-officer am jes got no heart. I begged an' begged: no use. Squire Johnson, he got his arms full, an' Miss Summer's a dozen. I tried to steal one, but he jes keep his eye onto me all de time. No use, no use.

JESSIE. Oh! what can have become of him?

STUB. Dunno', Miss Jessie. He was jes de bes' feller, was Massa Harry; an' now he's gone an' done somfin', I know he has. When de cap'n what picked me up in ole Virginny, in de war, — when he was a-dying in de horse-fiddle, says he to me, says he, Stub, I'm a-gwine ; an' when I's gone, you jes get up Norf. You'll find my brudder Harry up dar, an' you jes stick as clus to him as you's stuck to me, an' you'll find friends up dar. An' when it was all ober, here I come. An', Miss Jessie, I lub Massa Harry almos' as much as I did de cap'n; an' I'd do any ting for him an' you, who he lub so dearly.

JESSIE. I know you would, Stub. Heaven only knows when he will return to us. If he comes not soon, my heart will break. (*Weeps; goes and sits on bench.*)

STUB. Pore little lamb! She wants a letter: she shall hab one too. Massa Harry won't write: den, by golly, I'll jes make up a special mail-train, an' go down dere to de city, an' fotch one. It's jes easy 'nuff to slip down dere, an' hunt Massa Harry up, an' I'll do it. Say nuffin' to nobody, but slip off to-morrow mornin' an' hunt him up. (*Exit R., I.E.*)

KITTY (*comes down from gate*). Jessie, here's a surprise. Mr. Thornton is coming up the road.

JESSIE (*springing up*). Mr. Thornton? Heaven be praised! News of Harry at last! (*Runs up to gate, meets* MR. THORNTON, *takes his hand; they come down.*) O Mr. Thornton! Harry, what of Harry?

THORNTON. Miss Jessie, I am the bearer of bad tidings. Would it were otherwise!

JESSIE. Is he dead? Speak: let me know the worst; I can bear it.

THORNTON. Be quiet, my child. He is not dead; better if he were, for death covers all the evils of a life, — death wipes out all disgrace.

JESSIE. Disgrace? Oh, speak, Mr. Thornton! why is he silent? what misfortune has befallen him?

THORNTON. The worst, Jessie. Perhaps I should hide his wretched story from you; but I'm here to tell it to his friends, and you are the dearest, the one who trusted him as none other can. Jessie, the man you loved has been false to you, to all. He has abused the trust I placed in him. He has become a spendthrift, a libertine, a gambler, and a drunkard.

JESSIE. I will not believe it: 'tis false. Harry Maynard is too noble. Mr. Thornton, you have been misled, or you are not his friend.

THORNTON. I was his friend till he betrayed and robbed me. I am his friend no longer. Jessie, you must forget him; he will never return to his old home, his first love. He has broken away from my influence: he associates with the vilest of the vile, and glories in his shame.

JESSIE. Stop, stop! I cannot bear it.

THORNTON. Jessie, you know not how it pains me to tell you this; but 'tis better you know the worst. I have striven hard to make his path smooth, — to make his way to fortune easy, for your sake, Jessie. For I, — yes, Jessie, even in this dark hour I must say it, — I love you, as he never could love.

JESSIE. You — love — me? You! Oh! this is blasphemy at such a time.

THORNTON. I could not help it, Jessie. (*Tries to take her hand.*)

JESSIE. Do not touch me. I shall hate you. Leave me. O Harry, Harry! are you lost to me forever? (*Staggers up and sits on bench.*)

THORNTON (*aside*). I've broken the ice there. Rather rough; but she'll get over it. Now for old Maynard. I'd sooner face a regiment; but it must be done. (*Exit into house.*)

KITTY (*comes down to* JESSIE). O Jessie, this is terrible!

JESSIE. Don't speak to me, Kitty: leave me to myself. I know you mean well, but the sound of your voice is terrible to me.

KITTY (*comes down*). Poor thing! Who would have believed that Harry Maynard could turn out bad? I wish I could do something to help her. I can, and I will too. Oh, here's Tom! (*Enter* TOM *from house; sees* KITTY, *stops, then sticks his hat on one side; crosses to* L. *whistling.*)

KITTY. Tom!

TOM (*turns*). Eh! did you speak, Miss Corum?

KITTY. Yes, I did. Come here — quick — why don't you pay attention?

TOM. Didn't you forbid any further attention?

KITTY. Pshaw! no more of that! Do you remember what I told you my husband must be?

TOM. Yes: a sort of salamander to rush into burning

3

houses, an amphibious animal to save people from drowning.

KITTY. Ahem! Tom, to save people: just so. Well, Tom, you can be that hero, if you choose.

TOM. Me? How, pray?

KITTY. Harry Maynard has got into trouble in the city; he's a drunkard and a gambler, and every thing that is bad.

TOM. You don't mean it!

KITTY. It's true. Now, he must be saved, brought back here, or Jessie will die. Tom, go and find him, and when you come back, I'll sacrifice myself.

TOM. Sacrifice yourself?

KITTY. Yes, marry you.

TOM. You will consider him found. O Kitty, Kitty, — but hold on a minute. Have you given Nat Harlow a chance to be a hero?

KITTY. No, Tom: I'm serious now. Find Harry Maynard, and you shall be my hero.

TOM. Hooray, Kitty: tell me all about it. I'll be off by the next train. Come (*gives her his arm*), I can't keep still: I must keep moving. (*Exeunt* L.)

JESSIE. Lost! lost to me, and I loving him so dearly! You must forget him! He said forget: it is impossible. He loved me so dearly, too, before he left this house in search of fortune. No, no: I will not give him up; there must be some way to save him. If I only knew how! O Harry, Harry! why do you wander from the hearts that love you? Come back, come back! (*Covers her face and weeps. Enter* CHARITY GOODALL *from* R., *through gate.*)

CHARITY. Oh, this is delicious! I've climbed fences, torn my way through bushes, and had the most delightful frolic with Farmer Chips's little Chips on the hay, with nobody to check my fun and remind me of the proprieties of life. Ha, ha, ha! How my rich neighbor, Mrs. Goldfinch, would stare to see me enjoying myself in the coun- -try! Little I care! I shall go back with a new lease of life, a harvest of fresh country air, that will last me through the winter. (*Sees* JESSIE.) Hey-day, child, what's the matter? (*Sits beside her.*)

JESSIE (*flinging her arms round* CHARITY'S *neck*). O Aunt Charity! Harry, Harry—

CHARITY. Ah! the truant's heard from at last; and not the most delightful tidings, judging by your tear-stained cheeks. Well, child, tell me all about it.

JESSIE. He's lost to us. He has fallen into temptation; he's —

CHARITY. The old story. "A certain man went down unto Jericho, and fell among thieves."

JESSIE. O Aunt Charity, how can you be so heartless!

CHARITY. Heartless, Jessie! You must not say that. You know not my story. Listen to me. One I loved dearer than life was ingulfed in this whirlpool. He was a brave, noble fellow, who took a poor country girl from her home, and made her the mistress of a mansion, rich in comfort and luxury. For years our life was one of happiness; and then a friend, a false friend, Jessie, led him into temptation, with the base hope of securing his riches by his ruin. The friend failed to acquire the one, but wrought the other. He died ere he had become the wretched sot he hoped to make him; died in my arms, loving and repentant. I had his fortune, but my life was blighted. I refused to be comforted until the wretchedness about me brought me to my senses. Then I sought in work, strong, earnest work, consolation for my bereavement. With his wealth, I sought out the wretched, the outcasts of society; gave my aid to all good work, and so earned the title of a strong-minded woman. 'Tis often spoken with a sneer, that title, Jessie; but they who bear it have the world's good in their heart, thank Heaven for them all! And so I go about doing all I can to relieve distress, the surest solace for sorrow, Jessie; for there's nothing so cheering, as relieving the wretchedness of others. So don't call me heartless, Jessie.

JESSIE. O Aunt Charity, he was so good! he loved me so dearly!

CHARITY. And he has fallen. Who told you this?

JESSIE. His friend Mr. Thornton: he is here now, speaking with father. O dear aunt! can nothing be done to save him?

CHARITY. Thornton? What Thornton? Speak, Jessie, who is he?

JESSIE. Here comes Mr. Thornton. I will not see him. He has spoken to me of love, — his love for me, almost in the same breath in which he told of Harry's ruin. Oh, let me go! I can not, will not meet him. (*Runs off* L.)

CHARITY. So, so: the friend of Harry makes love to his wife that is to be, and his name is Thornton. I am curious to see this *friend.* (*Enter* THORNTON *from house.*)

THORNTON. That job's over. Now for Miss Jessie. (CHARITY *rises*.) Charity Goodall!

CHARITY. Yes, Charity Goodall, widow of Mark Goodall, your friend, Robert Thornton.

THORNTON (*aside*). What fiend sent her here to blast my well-laid plans?

(*Capt. Bragg appears* R., *and leans on the fence. He is a little tipsy. No Toodles business*).

CHARITY. So, sir, you are the friend of my nephew, Harry Maynard? here on a mission of mercy, to break gently to his sorrowing friends the news of his downfall?

THORNTON. 'Tis true.

CHARITY. And to console his affianced wife with the proffer of your affection.

THORNTON. 'Tis false!

CHARITY. It is the truth. I know you, Robert Thornton. Your work made my life a burden. You robbed me of one I loved; and now you have wound your coils about another victim.

THORNTON. You are mistaken: I sought to keep him from temptation; but he was reckless, and forsook me.

CHARITY. Where is he now?

THORNTON. I know not; neither do I care. He robbed me; and, were he found, I should give him up to justice.

CHARITY. Staunch friend indeed! He robbed you? I do not believe it. I have cause to mistrust you. I never dreamed you were the friend of Harry. But now I can see your wicked scheme. You have him in your power, but beware! My mission is to save. (*Goes up* R.)

THORNTON (*coming to* L.). Too late, too late. I do not fear you.

MAYNARD (*outside,* R.). Say no more: I will not seek him. (*Enter from house, followed by* MRS. MAYNARD.)

MRS. MAYNARD. O John, don't say that! He is our only boy.

MAYNARD. He has disgraced the name of Maynard. I will not seek, I will never allow him to cross my threshold. He went out a man: he shall never return a brute. (*Enter* CAPT. BRAGG, R., *through gate*.)

CAPT. Now, done yer say that, Maynard (hic). It's disgrace-ful to drink. I mean to get full. I never got full. I can drink a gallon, an' walk straight, I can (hic). But I'm a Bragg. I'm Cap'en Bragg of the Horse Marines; no, the

ill-ill-lus'rus Lawless Rangers, every man — full — full —
six — Now look a' here, look a' me, if your son's gone
to the dogs, don't you give him up. Look a' me. I'm
Bragg. I had a son : you know him : went off twenty years
ago. Do I give him up? Not a bit of it (hic). He'll come
back one of these days, rolling in his carriage ; I mean in
wealth. But then, he's a Bragg. We can't all be Braggs.
Come, le's go down, and hunt him up. I know all the places.

MAYNARD. Not a step will I stir. (*Enter* JESSIE, L.)
He has made his bed: let him sleep in it. He shall not disgrace my house with his presence.

JESSIE (*runs to him, falls on her knees*). No, no, father:
don't say that. You will not cast him off. Think what a
kind son he was : how he loved us all. You will try to save
him, father ! Don't say you will not ; my heart will break.

MAYNARD. Jessie, you know not how low he has fallen.
My son of whom I was so proud ! He has disgraced
his home. Henceforth he is no longer son of mine.· I will
not seek him. I have said it, Jessie, and John Maynard
never breaks his word.

JESSIE (*crosses to* MR. THORNTON). O Mr. Thornton !
you will seek him : you will save him for my sake?

THORNTON. He is past redemption. 'Twere useless.

JESSIE. Then I will go in search of him.

MAYNARD. You, Jessie?

JESSIE. Yes, I. He saved me, when a babe, from the
pitiless storm ; now I will seek him.

THORNTON. This is folly. He lurks with the vile and
worthless, in dens of filth and vice. Who will lead you there?

CHARITY (*comes down* C.). I will.

JESSIE (*rises and runs into her arms*). O Aunt Charity !

CHARITY. Yes, I. When man shrinks from the work
of salvation, let woman take his place. Look up, child !
Foul treachery has insnared him. From the toils of the
false friend, from the crafty arts of the boldest of schem-
ers, we will snatch him : from the depths of despair, we will
save him. Past redemption, Robert Thornton? False !
While there is life, there is hope !

(CHARITY *with her arms about* JESSIE, C. THORNTON,
L.; CAPT. BRAGG, L. C.; MAYNARD, R. C.; MRS. MAY-
NARD, R. TOM *and* KITTY *come on* R., *and stand behind
fence, looking on, quietly.*)

3*

SCENE. — *An elegant drinking-saloon. In flat,* R. *and* L., *arched doorways, with steps leading up and off* R. *and* L. ; *between these a mirrored door, closed, opening to* L., *and showing, when open, steps leading up over archway,* L. *Over arch the flat is painted on gauze for illumination. Three steps leading up to door,* C., *being a part of the steps that lead off* R. *and* L. ; *the whole flat handsomely gilded. Bar running up and down stage,* R. ; *behind bar, a handsome side-board, with decanters, glasses, and the usual paraphernalia of a bar-room. Table,* L. C., *with two chairs ;* L. *of table a lounge, on which* TOM LARCOM *is stretched, apparently asleep.* THORNTON R., *and* MURDOCK L. *of table, seated, bottle and glasses before them.* DALEY *behind bar, and two gentlemen, well dressed, standing before it, drinking. After* THORNTON *speaks they exit* R., *up steps.*

MURDOCK. Thornton, you have a princely way of doing things, and the luck of the evil one himself.

THORNTON. Shrewdness, old fellow. I'm an old hand at this sort of business, and glitter and dash go a long way in sharpening the appetites of one's customers.

MURDOCK. There's something more than glitter about this wine.

THORNTON. The wine is good, and costly too. Of course, I do not set this before everybody, or the profits would hardly come up to my expectation. I never throw pearls before swine. Home-made wares pay the best profit.

MURDOCK. Ah ! you do a little in the way of doctoring ?

THORNTON. A great deal, Murdock. I have a very

30

good dispensary close at hand, and Maynard has made himself decidedly useful in that branch.

MURDOCK. Maynard? is that miserable sot of àny use to you now?

THORNTON. Oh, yes! I alone can control him. Poor devil! he's breaking up fast. It's a pity such a likely young fellow could not let rum alone; but he would drink, and will until the end comes. 'Twill not be long.

MURDOCK. Where do you keep him? I've not seen him about to-night.

THORNTON. Close by, but out of sight. Some of his friends, a few months ago, made a demonstration towards his rescue from the pit into which he had fallen. I believe they are now searching high and low for him.

MURDOCK. An idle task, while he is in your clutches.

THORNTON. You're right, Murdock: he stood between me and the dearest wish of my life. Meddling fools thwarted me in that; and now, from sheer revenge, I'll hold him from them all.

MURDOCK. I'd rather have you for a friend than an enemy. (*Rising.*) Good-night. I must look after my own humble quarters. Ah! if I could only have your dash!

THORNTON. There's money in it, Murdock. (*Rises.*)

MURDOCK. I believe you: good-night.

THORNTON. Good-night: drop in again. (MURDOCK *goes up and off* R., *up steps.*) Daley, who's that on the lounge?

DALEY (*comes from behind bar*). I don't know him: he dropped in an hour ago, took a drink, and rolled on to the lounge.

THORNTON. Well, rouse him up, and get him out: that don't look respectable. (*Goes behind bar, and looks about.*)

DALEY (*goes to* TOM, *and shakes him*). Come, friend, rouse up. (*Another shake.*) Do you hear? rouse up!

TOM (*slowly rises and looks at him*). Rouse up? wha's that (hic)? No, le's fill up; that's besser (hic).

DALEY (*shaking him*). Well, get up; you're in the way.

TOM (*sitting up, and looking at him*). Say, wha's (hic) yer name?

DALEY. My name's Daley.

TOM. Daily (hic) what? Times? Oh, I know: you're a (hic) newsboy (hic), you are. Don't want no papers. (*Attempts to lie down again.*)

DALEY. Come, come, this won't do. Get up, I say !

TOM. I always take (hic) my breakfast in bed.

DALEY. You'll take yourself out of this ! (*Gets him on to his feet.*)

TOM. Wh- (hic) what you say, Mister Times ? Say (hic), le's drink !

DALEY. No: it's time you were home.

TOM. Home (hic)? wha's that? Fools a (hic) to this ? (*Staggers across, and clutches bar.*) I'm goin' t'stay (hic) here forever and always (hic), forever.

THORNTON. Oh, get him out, Daley !

TOM. Yes, get me out, Daily, for (hic) exercise. Take the air (hic). Air's good ; le's have some sugar (hic)in mine. (*Gets down,* R. ; *aside, sobered.*) So he's here, — Maynard is here. I've run the fox to earth at last. (*As before.*) Fetch on the drinks, D-Daily (hic) and a little oftener.

DALEY. Here's your hat,; come. This way, this way. (*Leads him up to steps,* R.)

TOM (*at steps, turns round*). Hole on a minute, D-Dai- (hic) ly ; give us your hand, D-Daily. I'll be back soon (hic), an' we'll never (hic), never (hic) part any more (hic). Good mornin', D-D-aily (hic), good morn. (*Exit up steps.* THORNTON *comes down to table,* L. ; DALEY *takes bottles and glasses from table and goes behind bar. Two gentlemen enter,* R., *drink, and go off.*)

THORNTON (*sits at table*). The luck of the evil one ! Murdock is but half right. The loss of that girl is a stroke of ill-fortune that imbitters all my prosperity. Get your supper, Daley ; I'll look after the bar. (DALEY *exits,* R., *up steps.*) But for the interference of Charity Goodall, she would have been mine. They have not found the missing Maynard yet. I have him safe : he cannot escape me. (*Soft music. The mirrored door, between entrances in flats, slowly opens, and* HARRY MAYNARD, *shrinking and trembling, with feeble steps, comes down, closing the door behind him. He creeps down to* THORNTON'S *chair.*)

HARRY. Thornton, Thornton !

THORNTON (*turns with a start*). You here ? '

HARRY (*trembling*). Yes, yes ; don't be fierce, don't. It is so dark and dismal up there ! and the rats — oh, such rats ! — glare at me from their holes. I couldn't stay. Don't send me back : I'll be very quiet. I'm sober too. Not a drop for two days : not a drop.

THORNTON. What's the matter with you now ?

HARRY. Oh! nothing, nothing: only I wanted to be sociable (*tries to smile*), — as sociable as you and I were in the old times.

THORNTON. Sociable! you and I! Bah! you're shaking like an aspen. What friendship can there be between me and a miserable sot like you?

HARRY. Yes, I know I'm not the man I used to be: I know it. Oh, the thought of that other life I lived once, tortures me almost to madness!

THORNTON. Well, why don't you go back to it?

HARRY. Back? back to that old home among the hills from which I came, full of lusty manhood? Back to the old man who looked upon me with all a father's pride? the dear mother whose darling I was? the fair, young girl whose heart I broke? Back there, with tottering steps, a pitiful wreck, to die upon the threshold of the dear old home? No, no: not that, not that!

THORNTON. Then be quiet. You have brought ruin upon yourself: you can't complain of me.

HARRY. No, I don't complain. It was a fair picture of fame and fortune you laid before me; and when I found the *honorable* mercantile business, in which you had amassed wealth, was work like this, I should have turned back.

THORNTON. I told you to keep a clear head and a steady hand; to *sell*, not poison yourself with my liquid wares.

HARRY. Yet you placed pleasures before me that turned my head, and —

THORNTON. They never turned mine. You were a fool, and fell.

HARRY. Ay, a fool! Yes, your fool, Robert Thornton. I quaffed the ruby wine, I flung myself into every indulgence, because you led me. I must keep a cool head and a steady hand, with fire in my veins! I feel I am condemned. Of my own free will, I flung away a life. I do not complain; but, when we stand before the last tribunal, Heaven be the judge if your hands are unstained with my life-blood, Robert Thornton.

THORNTON. Enough of this: back to your den.

HARRY. No, no, Thornton, not there! I will be quiet, silent; but do not, in mercy, do not drive me back there!

THORNTON. Poor devil! Well, stay here: look after the bar until Daley returns. (*Aside, going* L.) He can't resist: he'll make a dive for the brandy, and forget. Two days without it: I should not have allowed that. (*Exit* L., I.E.)

HARRY. Stay here! No, no, he has given me a chance for freedom. The doors are open: a dash, and I am free. Free for what? To die in the gutter. I could drag myself no farther; and who would look with compassion on such a ragged, bloated wretch as I? No, no: I have sold myself, body and soul, to this accursed life. (*Staggers to bar.*) Let me get at the brandy; that, at least, will bring freedom, — freedom from this maddening thirst, these horrible fears that drive me mad. (*Staggers behind bar.*) Ah, here, here! (*Seizes decanter.*) The balm for bitter memories. Stop, stop! That vision in the night, — Jessie, with her warning finger: and the old melody I loved so well rang in my ears. I vowed I'd drink no more, though I should die of madness. (*Buries his face in his arms upon the bar. Enter* R., *down steps*, CAPT. BRAGG.)

CAPT. Found a new place. (*Looking about.*) Superb — gorgeous — dazzling! Here's juiciness! Just my idea of a palace. The man who figured this place no doubt believes his plan original. Absurd! I planned it years ago. Bragg's plan stolen! Fact, by jingo! (*Raps on bar.*) Come, young man, business, business. (HARRY *raises his head:* BRAGG *staggers back.*) Harry Maynard, or I'm no Bragg! (*Comes to bar, and offers his hand.*) Harry, young fellow, how are you? (HARRY *falls back, and glares at him.*) Don't know me, hey? Why, I'm Bragg, Capt. Bragg, your distinguished townsman; Bragg of the Rangers; every man a sharpshooter, and their commander — well, modesty forbids my mentioning him in fitting panegyrics. Why, how you stare! You don't look well.

HARRY. I don't know you.

CAPT. Won't do, my boy, won't do. You may be able to bluff common folks, but I'm Bragg; Bragg of the judicial brow, Bragg of the penetrating eye: it's a keen one, and, when I fixed that detective's orb upon you, I said, There's my man! Why, they've fitted out an exploring party for the purpose of hunting you up, — Mrs. Charity Goodall, Jessie, Tom Larcom, and that black imp Stub. They've scoured the city in vain. They didn't ask my help, and I am the keen-eyed volunteer that never misses his mark. I have found you. Oh, here's glory, for Bragg's outwitted 'em all! I knew I should: Bragg never fails, never; and now I've got you, you can't escape me. Come, come, don't glare like a madman. What will I have? Brandy, of course! (HARRY *sets decanter and glass before him.*) They made a mistake: when there's any detective business to be done, call a Bragg. He can see farther and run faster than the sharpest of 'em. Fact, by jingo. (*Pours liquor into glass.*) Ah, that's my style! (*Raises glass.*) Here's to the glorious Rangers, Bragg's own!

HARRY (*excitedly*). Stop! don't drink that. See, there's a snake twisting and turning about in the glass. Stop, or you are a dead man!

CAPT. (*sets down glass, and staggers back*). Jersey light-ning!

HARRY (*glaring*). See, it's raising its head, — it will strike deep and sure: and there's another, and another. Look, they are crawling about the decanter: now they drop upon the bar: they are upon you: tear them off, tear them off! They strike and kill, strike and kill!

CAPT. He's raving mad. I wish I was well out of this.

HARRY. Thicker and thicker, faster and faster, they come upon the bar. See them glare at me! Back, back! (*Dashes his hands upon bar.*) Ah, they coil about my arms. Away, away! (*Attempts to tear them off.*) They crawl about me: they are at my throat. Help, help, help! (*Runs into* c., *and falls upon floor.*)

CAPT. He's got 'em bad. (*Runs to entrance,* R.) Fight 'em, young man, fight 'em: it's your only chance. I guess I won't drink: can't stop. (*Runs up and off,* R.)

HARRY (*raises his head*). Gone, gone at last with him. I've driven them off again; but they will come again. What's that? (*Glares into corner,* L.) Rats again: fierce and big! how they look at me! Away! Gleaming teeth and eyes of fire! Away, I say! I cannot drive them back. They swarm about me: they're at my legs. (*Tears them off.*) Devils, I'll fight you all! Closer and closer! (*Gets to his feet.*) They're making for my throat: away, I say! (*Tears them from his breast.*) I cannot, cannot. Now they're at my throat! (*Hands at his throat.*) Off, devils; off, I say! Help, help! oh, help! (*Falls quivering upon the stage. Enter* THORNTON, L.)

THORNTON. What's this, Maynard? Maynard, I say! (*Drags him to his feet.*)

HARRY (*clinging to* THORNTON). Don't let them get at

me : there's a thousand of them thirsting for my life. Save
me from them !

THORNTON.   Oh, you've been dreaming ! you're all right
now.   Come, get to bed : you'll sleep it off.   Up above
you're safe enough. (*Drags him up stage.*)

HARRY.   Not there, not there, Thornton.   Don't thrust
me into that hole to-night.   They're up there, lurking in
corners, waiting to eat me.   Don't, Thornton, don't !

THORNTON (*struggling with him*).   Fool, do as I bid you !
(*Throws open mirrored door.   STUB comes down steps, L.,
and watches them.*)

HARRY.   Not to-night, Thornton, not to-night ! (THORN-
TON *pushes him in, closes door, and locks it.   STUB comes
down softly, and sits L. of table.*)

THORNTON.   He's safe there.   I shouldn't wonder if
this night rid me of him.

STUB (*aside*).   Shouldn't wonder a bit.   (*Raps on table.*)
Here, bar-keeper, innholder, porter, bootblack, somebody or
anybody, am a genblem gwine to wait all night ? am he,
say, somebody ?

THORNTON.   Hallo ! who are you ?

STUB.   Hallo, yourself : a genblem widout extinction ob
color.   Hop beer and peppermint for one.   Be libely, be
libely !

THORNTON.   We don't serve niggers here.

STUB.   Wh-wh-what dat ?   Wha's yer ignorance ? wha's
yer ignorance ?   Take keer, take keer : five hundred dollars
fine !   Cibil rights bill : dat's me.   You can't fool dis
yer citizen widout extinction ob color : no, sir. (*Raps on
table.*)   Ginger ale and sassaparilla for one.   Be libely !

THORNTON.   Take yourself off : you cannot be served
here.

STUB.   Take keer, take keer ; don't elebate my choler :
don't rouse de slumbrin' African lion ; ef yer does, down
goes de whole hippodrome.   Don't cibil rights bill say, don't
he, ebery citizen, widout extinction ob color, am entitled to all
de privileges ob trabel, — de smokeolotive, steamboat, and
— and horse cars : an' to be taken in to all de inns, an' giben
all de freedom, — free lunch, free drinks, an' five hundred
dollars out ob de pocket ob any man dat says, Dry up ?
Dat's de law, mind yer eye. (*Raps on table.*)   Soda and
sassafras.   Be libely, be libely !

THORNTON (*takes a revolver from his pocket*).   Will you
have my pocket flask ?

STUB. O Lor! (*Slides under table.*) Dat ain't de kind : put 'im up, put 'im up! Ain't dry : guess I won't drink.

THORNTON. Out of this, or you'll get a taste of civil rights that will teach you better manners.

STUB. I's gwine : don't want no manners. (*Creeps out, and goes up stage. Enter* CHARITY GOODALL, R., *down steps, enveloped in a waterproof cloak : she comes down* C.)

THORNTON. What want you here? Who are you?

CHARITY (*extending her hand*). Charity.

THORNTON (*turning to table, and laying down pistol*). Away : you'll get nothing here !

CHARITY (*throws off cloak*). Don't be too sure of that, Robert Thornton.

THORNTON (*turns quickly*). Charity Goodall! (STUB *comes down softly, takes pistol, goes up, crosses stage, and hides behind bar.*) I beg your pardon, Mrs. Goodall. This is indeed a surprise !

CHARITY. And yet you have been expecting me ; dreading the hour when you and I should meet face to face.

THORNTON. This is hardly the place for a woman who would guard her good name from scandal.

CHARITY. You forget I am a woman above suspicion : that I have won a good name, by daring to enter such dens as yours, on errands of mercy.

THORNTON. Ah! indeed! what errand of mercy brings the saintly Charity Goodall into my humble saloon ?

CHARITY. Ah, you confess ownership ! The spider of the gilded web ! You, who, under the guise of a gentleman, lured my husband from an honorable life : you, who, with flattering promises of honorable wealth, tricked a brave lad to his ruin. Your humble saloon ! You sneer, and yet you tremble. Confess all : confess you are a villain and a cheat !

THORNTON. I will not listen to you. Be warned in time : at any moment, a rude throng may burst upon you. You are liable to insult from which I could not protect you.

CHARITY. Fear not for me : my mission is my protection. Alone, I have walked into the worst dens, without fear, without insult. With the most abandoned, no hand is raised against one who comes to rescue and deliver. Robert Thornton, listen to me : day and night I have sought, with ready helpers, Harry Maynard. To-night I have tracked him here.

4

THORNTON. Here?

CHARITY. Ay, here! You threw me from the scent with your story of his utter degradation. I never dreamed the silly fly was ensnared in the gilded web. Give him back to the friends who mourn for him, and, spite my wrongs, all shall be forgotten.

THORNTON. You ask too much: you see he is not here. You have been misinformed: for once the shrewd angel of mercy has been deceived.

CHARITY. Indeed! Perhaps another may be more successful — Jessie! (*Enter from* R., *hurriedly,* JESSIE.)

JESSIE. Have you found him? Speak! in mercy, speak!

CHARITY (*putting her arm about* JESSIE). Be calm, my child: there is the man who holds him in his power, — Robert Thornton.

JESSIE. Mr. Thornton? No, no, it cannot be! (*Falls on her knees to him.*) If you know where he is, if you can give him back to his father, to me, I will bless you.

THORNTON. You are mistaken, Jessie; I cannot give him back. You know how much I loved him. Think you, if it were in my power, I would refuse the request of the only woman I truly loved?

JESSIE. Oh, this is mockery! (*Rises, and goes to* CHARITY, *who folds her in her arms.*)

CHARITY. Poor child, your prayers are vain: that man is pitiless!

THORNTON. I told you you had been deceived. Was I not right? You tracked him here, and yet you cannot find him. See how your well-laid plan has failed!

CHARITY. No; for I have one resource left, one taught me by the noble women of the West. You fear for my good name: do you fear for those who come to my aid with the song he loved? Pray heaven it reach the prisoner's ear! (*Raises her hand. Chorus outside:* —

> "In the sweet by and by,
> We will meet on that beautiful shore," &c.

Enter, singing, from R. *and* L. *down steps, filling the steps, a chorus of women, well dressed, in light costumes; they stop upon the steps*)

HARRY (*above when the song ceases.*) Help, help! save, oh, save me!

JESSIE. His voice, Harry's voice! (*Kneels to* THORN-TON.) Man, now, if you have a spark of pity, lead me to him!

CHARITY. Robert Thornton, be merciful!

THORNTON. You plead in vain: he is beyond your reach.

STUB (*rising, behind bar*). Dat's a lie, dat's a lie! (*Runs up to door*, C., *and throws it open.*) Quick, Miss Jessie: he's up dar. Go fur him, go fur him! (*Steps* L.)

JESSIE. O Harry, Harry! (*Runs up steps, and exits through door.*)

THORNTON. Curse that fool: you must not enter there! (*Goes towards door.* CHARITY *runs up, closes door, and stands with back to it.*)

CHARITY. Back! you shall not enter here.

THORNTON. Woman, stand back: who shall prevent me? (STUB *steps before* CHARITY, *and presents pistol to* THORN-TON.)

STUB. Cibil rights bill: dat's me. (TOM *runs in from* R. *steps, and seizes* THORNTON'S *arms, binding them back.*)

TOM. Ha, ha! shrewdness, old fellow!

(*Lime light thrown on from* L., *above archway, showing* MAYNARD *extended on a low couch, resting on his right arm: dark pants, white shirt.* JESSIE *has her arm about him, supporting him*).

JESSIE. Harry, my own Harry, found at last!

HARRY. Jessie, Jessie, thank Heaven for this! (*Chorus:*

"In the sweet by and by," &c.

Repeated. Slow curtain.)

ACT IV. — THANKSGIVING AT THE OLD HOME.

SCENE. — *Interior of* JOHN MAYNARD'S *house. In flat,*
R. C., *bow-window, backed by road and trees, white with*
snow ; snow falling; door L. *Open fire-place,* R., *with*
bright fire; beside it, a high-backed seat for two; bureau
between door and window, in flat. Mantle over the fire-
place, with dried grasses in vases, clock, and other orna-
ments. Arm-chair L. ; *chair back of that. Door* R. U. E. ;
door L., *2d entrance.* MRS. MAYNARD *discovered at win-*
dow, looking out.

MRS. MAYNARD. The snow comes faster and faster.
It's time Stub was back from the depot with Charity. Ah,
'twill be a dull Thanksgiving for us this year: not like the
old times when we had Charley, Harry, and Jessie, to make
us all merry. Dear me ! time does break up households.
(*Enter* JOHN *from door* L.)

JOHN. I've put him on Harry's bed, mother. I expect
you'll scold when you see your white counterpane muddied
by his boots, for I couldn't get him beneath it. Poor devil !
I fear 'twill be his deathbed. I'd about made up my mind
that I'd never give another tramp shelter ; but he looked so
bad, I hadn't the heart to turn him away (*sits on bench*)
when I thought, mother, that our poor boy might have
come in the same way.

MRS. MAYNARD (*comes down*). That's so like you, John !
Is he very bad ?

JOHN. Yes : broken down with hunger and drink. He
begged hard for a little brandy. It was well I had none, for
'twould have been cruel to refuse him, and I would die ere I
touched the curse, the cause of so much misery to us.

40

MRS. MAYNARD. Ah, John, all that's over.

JOHN. Yes, mother, we must hope for the best. He was saved, thanks to Charity: but still I fear for him. 'Twill be a day to remember, when we have him back.

MRS. MAYNARD. A long, long year since Charity found him, and no word or sign from our loved one.

JOHN. Ah, mother, I like that: I was uncharitable, — I, who have been so bitter against others who turned their faces from the fallen. But I'm proud of *him*. "Tell father," he said to Charity, "tell him I will never cross his threshold till I can return as I went, — a man." That's so like a Maynard! that's the true grit: I like that.

MRS. MAYNARD. And Charity will give us no news of him.

JOHN. No: she shakes her head. "Give him time, give him time:" but she smiles when she says it; and, when Charity smiles, you can depend upon it all's going well. We must trust her, mother. So we have two more faces in the fire, Harry's and Jessie's. (*Sleigh-bells heard without.*) Ah! there she is, there she is! (*Goes to window.*) No, it's Tom and Kitty with the baby. Why, mother, they've brought the baby: here's a surprise for you.

TOM (*outside*). Whoa, I tell you! Give me the baby, Kitty: that's all right. Now come along, come along. (*Enters door in flat, with a baby well bundled in his arms.*)

JOHN. Tom, glad to see you: this is hearty. Come to the fire; and, Kitty, give us a smack. (*Kisses KITTY.*)

TOM. Hallo! easy there; but I suppose it's all right.

JOHN. Right? of course 'tis. Now give me the baby.

TOM. To serve in the same style? No, I thank you; it's a tenderer bit than Kitty.

KITTY. Tom, don't be silly!

MRS. MAYNARD. I'll take him, Tom, the little darling. (*Takes baby.*)

TOM (*reluctantly giving it up*). Certainly, only handle him gently: I'm terribly anxious.

MRS. MAYNARD (*sits on settle. JOHN helps KITTY off with her things*). Oh, you little beauty!

TOM (*leans on mantle, back, and watches her*). The picture of his daddy: that's what they all say. Is his nose all right? Ain't much of it, but, if the frost got at it, good-by nose. Take care! Oh, Lord, I thought you had dropped

4*

him. Hey, Johnny, look up : he's a smart one for a three-months' older. Hadn't I better take him?

KITTY. Tom, do you suppose Mrs. Maynard don't know how to handle a baby?

TOM. Well, I don't know, Kitty; they break awful easy. You just keep your eye on him until I put up the horse. (*Going; returns.*) Does he look all right, Mrs. Maynard?

MRS. MAYNARD. Right! don't you see he's wide awake?

TOM. Yes : but hadn't he ought to be asleep?

KITTY. Tom, do go and put up your horse. I never saw such a goose; when he's awake, you think he should be asleep, and when he's asleep you want to wake him.

TOM. Parental anxiety. You see, Mrs. Maynard, this is something new to me.

KITTY. Well, isn't it new to all of us? Do go along!

TOM. I'm off. (*Exit door in flat.*)

KITTY. Such a plague!

JOHN. Ah, Kitty, not satisfied! You regret not having taken the other, Nat Harlow.

KITTY. No, indeed. Tom's the best husband in the world. I've not heard a cross word from him the whole year since we've been married; but he does make such a fuss about baby! Sha'n't I take him, Mrs. Maynard?

JOHN. Oh, ho! somebody else makes a fuss too. (*Sleigh-bells heard.*) Ah, here's Charity at last.

CHARITY (*outside*). Drive to the barn, Stub; I'll jump out. (*Enters door in flat.*) Here I am, you dear old John. (*Shakes hands, and kisses* JOHN.)

JOHN. Welcome, Charity; a thousand times welcome!

CHARITY. I knew you'd be glad to see me. (*Runs to* MRS. MAYNARD, *and kisses her.*) You dear, dear old Hannah!

MRS. MAYNARD. Ah, Charity, you always bring sunlight with you.

CHARITY. A baby! bless me! Oh! it's yours, Kitty. That for you (*kisses her*), and this for the baby. (*Kisses baby.*)

KITTY. Young as ever, Mrs. Goodall. Come, Mrs. Maynard, let me carry the baby off to bed. Don't move : I know the way. (*Takes baby, and exits* R. U. E.)

JOHN. Now, Charity, our boy —

MRS. MAYNARD. Yes, Harry! What news?

CHARITY. Dear me! do let me get my things off. (*Re-*

moves cloak and hat. MRS. MAYNARD *takes them, and carries them off* R. U. E. CHARITY *sits, and looks into fire.*) What a glorious blaze! (JOHN *leans on back of bench.*) Ah, John, I've often envied you your quiet evenings here, with this for company; often seen you and Hannah sitting here together, taking so much comfort. (*Enter* MRS. MAYNARD, R. U. E., *and leans on bench, between* CHARITY *and the fire.*)

MRS. MAYNARD. O Charity! tell us of our boy.

JOHN. Yes, yes, Charity, be merciful: what of him?

CHARITY (*rises and comes* L.). Oh, do be patient! I've a strange fancy to see how you look there in the old seat. Come, take your places, and tell me what you see there. (JOHN *sits with* MRS. MAYNARD *on bench, she next the fire; he takes her hand.*) That's nice. (*Goes to back of bench.*) Now, tell me, what see you there? (*Enter* STUB, *door in flat, excitedly.*)

STUB. I've put 'em up, Miss Charity, an'— an'—

CHARITY. Silence, Stub! (*He comes down* L.)

STUB (*aside*). Dat's de quarest woman eber I see: ben in de house five minutes, an' not tole de news.

CHARITY. Well, John, I'm waiting.

JOHN. There, Charity, is my picture-gallery of old memories, that both sadden and cheer waiting and aching hearts. What do I see? (*Looking into fire.*) The face of my brave soldier boy: the face that has glowed upon us in its noble manhood for many, many years.

CHARITY. The face of a hero, John: there are no bitter memories there. He died bravely: passed into the better life with the grand army of martyrs, crowned with glory.

STUB. Yas indeed, dead an' gone, Massa Cap'n: God bless him! Miss Charity, am you gwine to tell—

CHARITY. Be silent! (STUB *goes* L., *shaking his head.*)

STUB. I shall bust it out: I can't help it.

CHARITY. Well, brother John.

JOHN. Another, a younger face. Now I see it with the glow of health upon the cheeks, the eye bright and laughing, as I have seen it come and go before me in the old days. And now—'tis pale and haggard: the eyes are bloodshot. O Charity, the face that has haunted my sleep! I have tried to shut it out; but it comes before me with a look full of reproach. Oh had I but been merciful, all this might not have been!

CHARITY. And yet that, too, is the face of a hero.

STUB. Oh! why don't she tell 'em?

CHARITY. Go on, John: look once more.

JOHN. Once more: the face of a fair, bright girl, who won her way to my heart. I never knew how much I loved, until I lost her. She left me, nobly left me: I had no right to stay her. Will she come back, Charity? will she?

STUB. Why, don't you know —

CHARITY. Silence, Stub! Now, brother John, let me tell you what I see there. I see the face of that same brave, true girl, in all its beauty: the girl who forsook home and friends, with the brave wish in her heart to save her lover from destruction. I see her gladly embracing a life of hard, grinding poverty, cheering the fainting spirit of a broken man, guarding and guiding him through the dark valley of remorse, until he stands alone, strong, resolute, determined.

JOHN. Jessie, our Jessie: well, well, go on.

CHARITY. I see her with the rich glow of health again mantling her cheeks: I hear the ringing laugh of the happy girl again: I see her returning to her father's house (*enter* JESSIE, *door in flat*), a proud, true, happy wife!

JESSIE (*running down to* JOHN). Here, here again: dear, dear father!

JOHN (*rising, and taking her in his arms*). Jessie, my darling, a thousand and a thousand times welcome!

JESSIE. Dear, dear mother, your child has returned to you.

MRS. MAYNARD (*takes her in her arms*). O Jessie, Jessie, welcome! do you come alone?

CHARITY. Be patient! sit you down and listen. (*They sit again,* JESSIE *kneeling between* MRS. MAYNARD *and the fire.*)

STUB. Wh-wh-what all dis mean? Ain't you gwine —

CHARITY. Silence, Stub! I see another face, — the face of the young man who went forth to fight the battle of temptation. I see him struggling: I see friends around him: I see one with a true, loving heart, clinging to him through good and evil report: see him fighting valiantly in the distant West: see the freshness of renewed life in his ruddy cheek, until, his foe beneath his feet, he comes back to his old home. (*Enter* HARRY, *door in flat.*)

JOHN (*rushing down* R.). I see it all, Charity: my boy has come home. Where, oh, where is he?

HARRY. Here, father, here.

JOHN (*turns*). O Harry, Harry! my dear, dear boy! (*Rushing into his arms.*)

STUB. Hi, golly! dat's de ticket, dat's de ticket!

HARRY. Mother, have you no word for the truant?

MRS. MAYNARD (*embracing him*). My heart is too full, Harry! (HARRY, C.; MRS. MAYNARD, R. C.; JESSIE, R.; MR. MAYNARD, L. C.; CHARITY, L.; STUB, *extreme* L.)

HARRY. Mother, father, of the bitter past —

JOHN. We'll not hear a word, Harry. We have you safe again: let the sorrows of the past be forgotten in the joy of the present. Mother, look at him! what a frame, what a face! Hang me, if I don't believe all this has been a joke!

HARRY. Nay, father, in remembering the trials we 'have passed, we gain new hope for the future. I am a free man, with a home of my own; rich Western lands own me as master; but I owe all to the dear girl who loved me, — the brave, noble woman who befriended me. Come here, little wife: let my parents see that the child they adopted is now theirs by right. (JESSIE *goes to him.*)

JESSIE. Yes, father, we ran away and were married: will you forgive us?

JOHN. Forgive you, puss? it was Harry's salvation! (*Enter* TOM, *door in flat.*)

TOM. There, the horse is all right: now for the baby. Bless my soul, where's the baby? (*Enter* KITTY, R. U. E.)

KITTY. Asleep, Tom; don't make such a noise!

TOM. Asleep! he'll die of starvation. Here! (*Takes nursing-bottle from his pocket.*) I forgot to leave his luncheon.

KITTY (*snatching bottle*). Tom, I'm ashamed of you, before all these folks! (*They go up. Enter* CAPT. BRAGG, *door in flat.*)

CAPT. Ah, Maynard, how are you? I just dropped in as I was going by. Why, bless my soul! Harry Maynard, as fresh as a buttercup! Why, how are you? and Jessie too! Well, this is glorious! (*Shakes hands.*) John, old friend, you're a lucky dog! I thought the boy was about gone, the last time I saw him; but he's come round all right. Ah! I always told you to keep up a stout heart! Look at me: I'm nearly seventy: my boy has been gone twenty years; but I know he'll come back, — come back a hero, or a millionnaire: he couldn't help it! he's a Bragg. He'll come back!

THORNTON (*outside*, L.). Away! away, you cannot reach

me: I defy you, I defy you! (*Rushes in* L., *and falls prostrate at* BRAGG'S *feet.*)

CAPT. (*shrinking back*). Hallo, what's this?

HARRY (*runs to* THORNTON, *and raises his head*). Merciful Heavens, 'tis Thornton!

ALL. Thornton!

THORNTON (*feebly*). Who said Thornton? What, Maynard! Maynard, you here?

HARRY. O Thornton! has it come to this?

THORNTON. Yes, Maynard, I'm down: down deeper than I had you. There's no hope! Only a year, only a year! I was cheated. I, who thought myself so shrewd and keen, in one night lost all, and took to drink. Oh, it's glorious to drown all trouble in the flowing bowl! Ha, ha! but it gets you at last: it has me. I have begged, cheated, stolen, for a single draught. Give me a drink: a drop of brandy, only a drop to cool my burning throat!

HARRY. You ask this of me, whom you so bitterly wronged?

THORNTON. Yes, I did wrong you; but I loved that girl as I loved but one other! Maynard, Maynard, hear me! this one woman I wronged: she haunts me: she was my wife. I forsook her, cast her off. She came from your native town. Her name — her name was — Alice Clarke.

JOHN. Alice Clarke — Jessie's mother!

THORNTON. Jessie's mother! No, no; don't tell me that: don't make me a greater villain than I know myself to be.

JOHN. She died beneath my roof, giving her child to my keeping.

JESSIE. He is my father: stand back! Harry, my place is here! (*Kneels, and supports him.*)

THORNTON (*looks in her face*). And I pursued you with a sinful love: brought *him* down to the very gates of death.

JESSIE. All is forgotten, all forgiven, father.

THORNTON. Take her away, take her away: I can't bear her touch! (*Crawls down stage.*) Her eyes glare at me! There's the look of her dead mother in them. Oh, spare me, spare me!

HARRY. O Thornton, Thornton, this is terrible!

THORNTON. Thornton! you're wrong. Call me by my rightful name: you must have heard it, — William Bragg.

JOHN. William Bragg?

CAPT. No, no; it cannot be! You, you my Bill? Curse you: you stole that name! That was my boy's, — a handsome, noble fellow!

THORNTON. I am your son!

CAPT. It's a lie: you're a miserable wretch! Think you a Bragg would come home in such a plight? I'll not believe it. (*Looks at him, then sinks on his knees, covers his face.*) It's false! I can not, will not believe it.

. THORNTON. You must, you do, old man. You might have made me a better man; but you nursed my vanity, and — well, well, it's all over now. I've dug my grave: let me rest in peace.

CAPT. (*rising to his feet*). No, no peace for you: you have disgraced my name. Die, die like a dog! Why did you come back here to ruin me, to drag me down from my position, to make me a by-word and a scorn among my neighbors? Why didn't you die in the gutters of your infamous city? But here, here! Die, but take my —

CHARITY (*puts her hand on his shoulder*). Pause ere you speak. He is dying; he has sinned: leave his punishment to a higher Power. Here, where our hearts are warm with gratitude for a blessed deliverance, curse not, but forgive as we all hope to be forgiven!

TABLEAU. — *With her left hand on his shoulder,* BRAGG *slowly sinks to his knees; her other hand is pointed up.* THORNTON *feebly raises his head, and follows her hand.* HARRY *sits in chair,* L., *with his arm about* JESSIE, *who kneels at his side, looking at* THORNTON; STUB *extreme* L. JOHN MAYNARD *with his wife stand* R., *2d entrance;* KITTY *on bench;* TOM *leaning on back of bench, looking at* THORNTON. *Slow curtain; music:* —

" In the sweet by and by," &c.